Idea #8,427
SKY SUIT
Wearable Weather Balloon

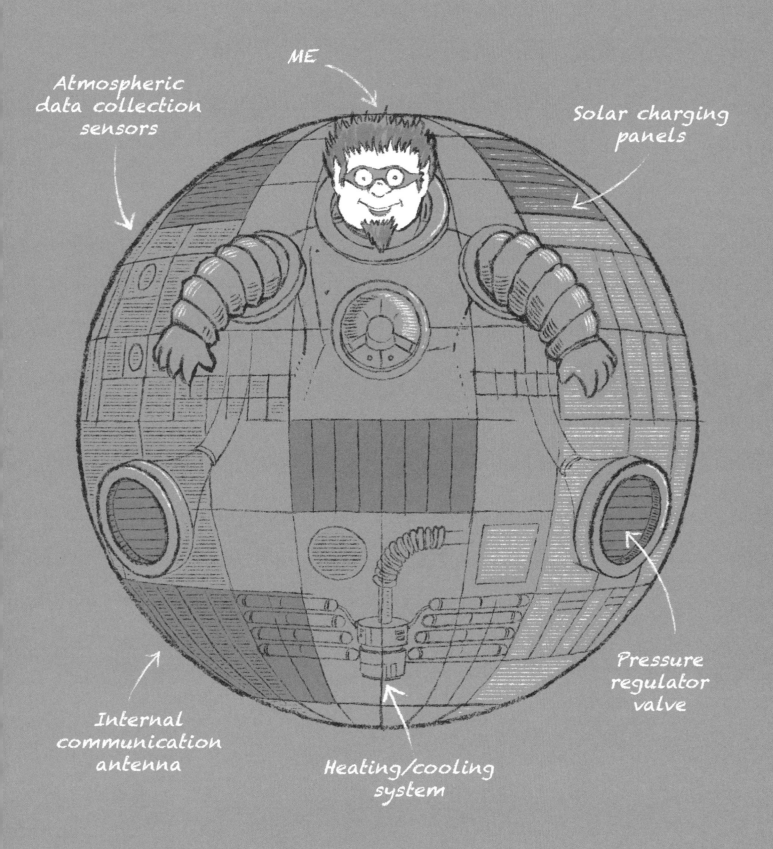

Atmospheric data collection sensors

ME

Solar charging panels

Internal communication antenna

Heating/cooling system

Pressure regulator valve

MAD SCIENTIST ACADEMY

THE WEATHER DISASTER
Peachtree

MATTHEW McELLIGOTT

CROWN BOOKS
FOR YOUNG READERS
NEW YORK

**To Christy and Anthony,
and to Emily Easton, editor extraordinaire**

ACKNOWLEDGMENTS
Special thanks to stratospheric meteorologist
Jason Gough for his expert advice and guidance

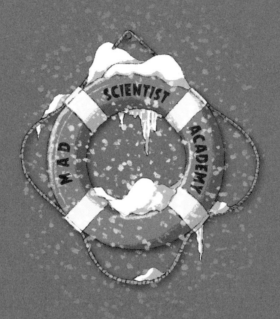

Visit us on the Web! randomhousekids.com

Educators and librarians, for a variety of teaching tools,
visit us at RHTeachersLibrarians.com

Library of Congress Cataloging-in-Publication Data
Names: McElligott, Matthew.
Title: The weather disaster / Matthew McElligott.
Description: First Edition. | New York : Crown Books for Young Readers, [2016] | Series: Mad scientist academy
Identifiers: LCCN 2015024027 | ISBN 978-0-553-52376-8 (hardback) | ISBN 978-0-553-52379-9 (glb) | ISBN 978-0-553-52380-5 (ebook)
Subjects: LCSH: Severe storms—Juvenile literature. | Storms—Juvenile literature. | Floods—Juvenile literature.
Classification: LCC QC941.3 .M44 2016 | DDC 551.55—dc23

The text of this book is set in Sunshine.
The illustrations were created with ink, pencil, and digital techniques.

MANUFACTURED IN CHINA
10 9 8 7 6 5 4 3 2 1
First Edition

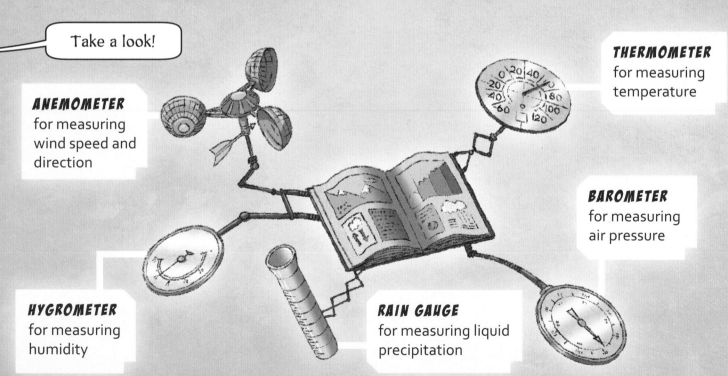

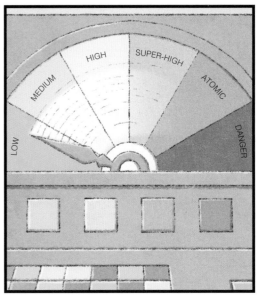

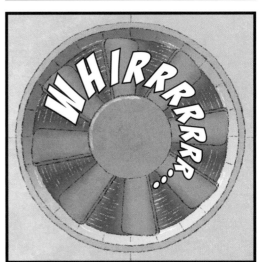

It's super cold up here by this vent.

It's really hot down here next to this vent.

So what does that tell you?

I get it! It's like Professor Nimbus said. The warm air is rising and the cool air is rushing down to take its place. That's making wind!

Exactly! But those vents shouldn't be blowing such different temperatures. There must be something wrong with the machine.

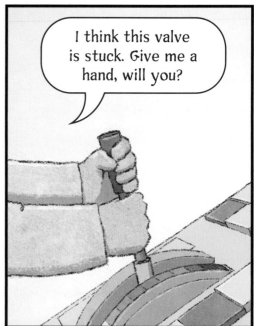

I think this valve is stuck. Give me a hand, will you?

CRACK!

Hmm. That seems to have made it worse.

BEEP! BEEP! BEEP! BEEP!

I'd better go get my repair kit. In the meantime, I'd like you all to check some other rooms in the school and see how the CHAOS machine is working.

Use your handbooks and take some measurements, then meet me back here.

Tad, Ken, and I will go to the greenhouse.

BEEP! BEEP! BEEP! BEEP! BEEP!

Nicole, Thora, and I will check out the pool.

Hey, Scarlet—the hygrometer shows the humidity is very high. There's a ton of water vapor in the air.

That makes sense. The handbook says that clouds form when warm, moist air rises and condenses.

THE WATER CYCLE

CONDENSATION

Cold temperatures higher in the atmosphere cause water vapor to condense into water droplets and ice crystals. This forms clouds.

EVAPORATION

Heat causes water vapor (moist air) to rise into the atmosphere.

PRECIPITATION

When so much water has condensed that the clouds cannot hold it anymore, the frozen or liquid water falls back to the earth.

If this condensation continues, it can even cause precipitation, like...

RAIN!

TYPES OF PRECIPITATION

COLD AIR	COLD AIR	COLD AIR	COLD AIR
WARM AIR	WARM AIR	WARM AIR	
		COLD AIR	
RAIN	**FREEZING RAIN**	**SLEET**	**SNOW**
Snow melts as it falls and turns into water droplets.	Snow melts, then freezes again when it hits the cold ground.	Snow melts, then freezes again before it hits the cold ground.	Snow stays frozen the whole time it falls.

Back in the greenhouse...

Can't see!

It's a flood! We should head back.

I'll try to find the door.

This way.

No. This way!

It's this way! Follow me!

Hurry!

I think it's locked. It won't open!

I open door!

HOW A THUNDERSTORM FORMS

COLD AIR

ELECTRICAL CHARGE

WARM AIR

When enough warm, moist air keeps rising into the path of a cold, dry air mass, it can form a thunderstorm.

Water droplets and ice pellets get tossed up and down inside the cloud. This forms an electrical charge.

If the charge gets strong enough, it can be released to the ground as a bolt of lightning.

It's getting worse. We have to stop it!

But how?

KA-BAM!

HOW A TORNADO FORMS

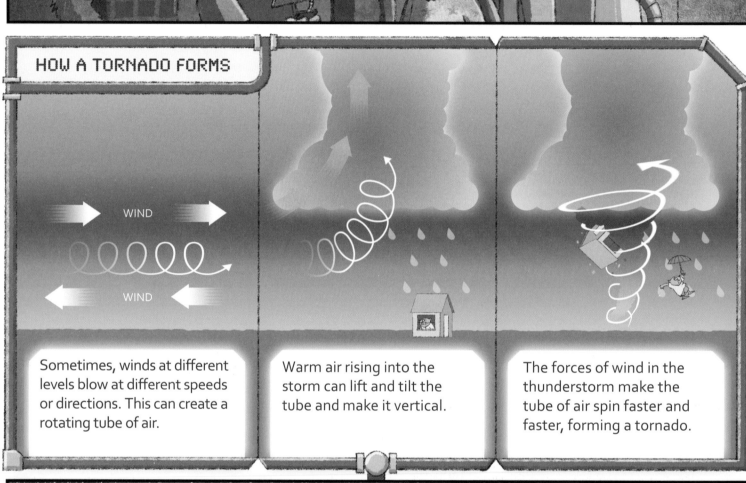

Sometimes, winds at different levels blow at different speeds or directions. This can create a rotating tube of air.

Warm air rising into the storm can lift and tilt the tube and make it vertical.

The forces of wind in the thunderstorm make the tube of air spin faster and faster, forming a tornado.

CLIMATE AND WEATHER

Dr. Cosmic,

Here are some notes about climate and weather you can share with your students.

—Prof. Nimbus

CLIMATE

CLIMATE IS THE AVERAGE PATTERN OF WEATHER IN A PLACE OVER MANY YEARS. FOR EXAMPLE, THE CLIMATE OF HAWAII IS WARM, BUT THE CLIMATE OF ANTARCTICA IS FREEZING COLD.

POLAR CLIMATE
(COOL TO VERY COLD ALL YEAR LONG)

TEMPERATE CLIMATE
(HOT IN SUMMER, COLD IN WINTER)

TROPICAL CLIMATE
(WARM TO HOT ALL YEAR LONG)

TEMPERATE CLIMATE
(HOT IN SUMMER, COLD IN WINTER)

POLAR CLIMATE
(COOL TO VERY COLD ALL YEAR LONG)

WEATHER SATELLITES

WEATHER SATELLITES ARE KEY TOOLS THAT SCIENTISTS USE TO STUDY WEATHER AND CLIMATE. THESE SPACECRAFT CIRCLE THE EARTH AND SEND BACK DATA ON CLOUDS AND STORMS, TEMPERATURES IN THE ATMOSPHERE, AND WIND SPEEDS.

For more weather facts, links, projects, and games, be sure to visit madscientistacademybooks.com.

WEATHER

WEATHER IS THE CONDITION OF THE ATMOSPHERE IN A PLACE OVER A SHORT PERIOD OF TIME. IT INCLUDES TEMPERATURE, WIND, CLOUDS, AND PRECIPITATION. WEATHER CAN BE VERY DIFFERENT IN NEARBY LOCATIONS ON THE SAME DAY. FOR EXAMPLE, IT MAY BE RAINING AT YOUR HOUSE, BUT SUNNY JUST A FEW MILES AWAY.

SUN	MON	TUE	WED	THU	FRI	SAT
82	86	84	81	80	84	87
60	63	61	58	57	60	63

Idea #8,513
CHAOS MACHINE
(Cooling/Heating Airflow Operating System)

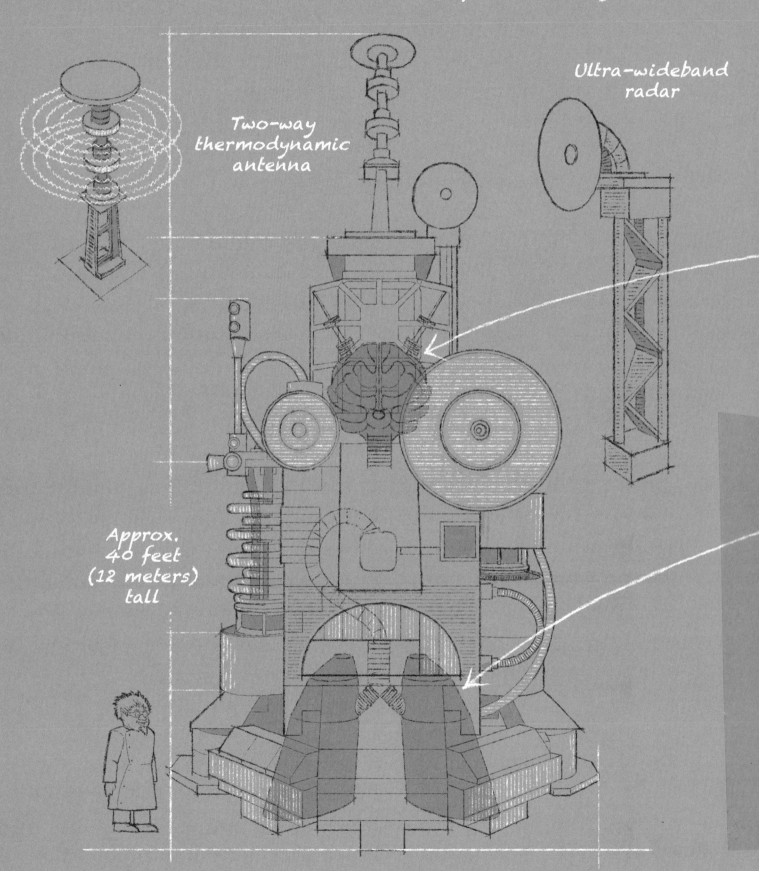

Two-way thermodynamic antenna

Ultra-wideband radar

Approx. 40 feet (12 meters) tall